Heather, Davy, and the Marshwiggle

Heather, Davy and the Marshwiggle

Dreamed by Lewis H. Diggs, III
Storyline by Gwendolyn B. Diggs And

Edited by

TERESSA L. DIGGS

ReadersMagnet, LLC

Heather, Davy, and the Marshwiggle
Copyright © 2024 by Teressa L Diggs

Published in the United States of America
ISBN   Paperback: 979-8-89091-577-1
ISBN   eBook: 979-8-89091-578-8

All rights reserved. No part of this publication may be reproduced, stored in a retrieval system or transmitted in any way by any means, electronic, mechanical, photocopy, recording or otherwise without the prior permission of the author except as provided by USA copyright law.

The opinions expressed by the author are not necessarily those of ReadersMagnet, LLC.

ReadersMagnet, LLC
10620 Treena Street, Suite 230 | San Diego, California, 92131 USA
1.619. 354. 2643 | www.readersmagnet.com

Book design copyright © 2024 by ReadersMagnet, LLC. All rights reserved.

Cover design by Jhie Oraiz
Interior design by Dorothy Lee

TABLE OF CONTENTS

Dedication 7
Chapter 1 - The Little Helpful Marshwiggles!..........................11
Chapter 2 - To the Cranberry Bogs 15
Chapter 3 - The Little Adventure 17
Chapter 4 - Oh, Come Find Us! 21
About the Author 27

DEDICATION

This book is dedicated to my late Father-in-law, Lewis Henry Diggs, III, of York, Pennsylvania. The Marshwiggles were brought to life by him and my Mother-in-law, Gwendolyn Bernice Diggs of Shippensburg, Pennsylvania as they drove the Pennsylvania countryside with their three children, Bruce, Valerie, and Lewes. The Marshwiggle stories would keep the three toddlers quiet and entertained in the car as the family would travel back and forth from Pennsylvania, while visiting family, to their own home in Hingham, Massachusetts.

When Lewis, better known as Grandee, was a youngster he loved to read the adventures of the Brownies by the Canadian Artist Palmer Cox which were created around the 1880's. Lew and Gwen would make up their stories of the Marshwiggles and, would often times, reminisce the adventures similar to the adventures they remembered from their reading the stories of Palmer Cox.

Grandee always wanted to have his Marshwiggles to come alive in a book and he even designed a pair of jeans with the

Marshwiggle logo on them that were worn by family members in Denver, Colorado. He hoped to have Gwen write the stories they told their toddlers and then publish them in a children's book. Gwen did put together a storyline in four short stories of the mischievous little Marshwiggles, but never got them published. They have been edited and recreated in this book, and three more to come, by me, Teressa Diggs. Grandee's dream is now a reality.

There are now many little Marshwiggles running around Atlanta, Georgia and Denver, Colorado and many cities in Wyoming that Grandee never got to meet and who never got to meet Grandee or Grandmother. This book is the first in the series to come alive for all those little Marshwiggles to enjoy. And I wanted to share with the world these fun adventures and the dreams of a brilliant man who tried so hard to get his story out but never could quite get it done.

Valerie gave her blessing to me to impart on this endeavor, as she is the only family member of the original bunch. She told me from her memories that there were two kids playing in the cranberry bog and one saw eyes looking at them. They ran to the area, but nobody was there, they kept going back and finally found the eyes, they belonged to a creature they never saw before but they weren't scared since it was so little. The creature came closer and told the two kids that he was a Marshwiggle and lived in the bog. They told him their names and they all played until the kids had to go home, but they played together every day after that.

Hopefully, you will like the adventures of the Marshwiggles as much now as Bruce, Valerie, and Lewes did way back then in the early 60's.

P.S.

A special thanks to my roommate and best friend, James Franklin Lee, for his encouragement and assistance in this endeavor. Without him, I would not have been able to make this dream come true. Thank you, James, and thank you all.

CHAPTER 1

The Little Helpful Marshwiggles!

"Tell us a story, Grandee," chirped little Davy as he tried to climb on the rocking chair on which Grandee was sitting.

"Okay, Okay, little monkey," laughed Grandee. "But first, get down."

"Yay," Davy jumped down and knelt on the floor near Grandee's chair. His sister Heather joined him at once.

Davy was a five-year-old boy with short, dark curls and dark eyes. Heather, his sister, was seven, with big eyes and pigtails. She was a bright and curious child who wanted to learn new things about the world around her.

Davy and Heather lived with their parents and Grandee in a small but beautiful house located on a huge farm near the outskirts of a little town.

Their father, Donte Washington, was an African American man in his 30s and their mother, Susan, was a Swedish woman with blonde hair and blue eyes. They had met a long time ago and were married soon enough.

Grandee looked so much like their Daddy, but he was in his sixties. He worked at the farm and loved telling children stories.

"So, what story should I tell you today?" Grandee tapped his index finger on his cheek, lost in his thoughts.

"The story about Marshwiggles," suggested Heather.

"But you have heard it already," frowned Grandee.

"Several times."

"I forgot it," pouted Davy, and Grandee shook with laughter.

"Alright then," he said.

The kids crossed their legs and sat up straight, with their eyes fixed on Grandee. They were ready for their story.

Grandee sighed and looked into the space for a brief moment before he began. When Grandee made up stories, he could tell everything in the story. Everything, just like you could if you made it up. But all he knew about Marshwiggles was that they lived next to the cranberry bogs, and they had golden eyelashes. They must be terribly shy because not many had seen them, and they were very quick – he thought he had seen one wiggle away once, but he really couldn't be sure.

"As far as we know about Marshwigggles, they are very diverse. They are dark-skinned, but some are white; you can even see some brown fellows amongst them.

Their eyes can be any color, but their golden eyelashes are long and thick," Grandee began.

"Don't you think their eyelashes are thick? With their size, they must be children. They are fast and smart. They can speak multiple languages and can tell the exact time by just looking at the sky. They have carved them an entire colony with markets, schools, and houses near the marsh."

"Tiny markets?" Heather was as intrigued as she was when she had first heard about the tiny people living somewhere around them.

"Ahaa," Grandee nodded his head.

"They know magic?" Heather confirmed, and Grandee nodded his head once again.

"Magical beings, very fascinating," Grandee sipped his cool dandelion wine.

"Please, tell us what happened to your friend, Grandee," asked Davy, who had just said he had forgotten the story. Grandee smiled at his little curious face.

"My friend Tyrone went to get some wood in the forest and got lost. As it got dark, he couldn't see anything and ended up falling into a dark pit in the middle of the forest. He got very scared thinking some animal might eat him," Grandee said.

"Then what happened?" Heather gulped.

"He called out for help and was almost hopeless when a tiny head poked above him. He couldn't believe his eyes, so he rubbed them hard and looked again. He wasn't dreaming. One after another, many small heads appeared above the pit and threw him a rope to help him come out." "Did he come out safely, Grandee?" Davy asked with his eyes as big as saucers.

"Yes, but once he came out, the tiny people were nowhere to be seen," Grandee said.

"Where had they gone?" Heather was confused.

"No idea; they disappeared in the cranberry bogs."

"Is that where they live?" Davy asked.

"I think so. Nobody knows where they live exactly, but what does it matter? We know they are real, and that's what we need to know," Grandee finished.

CHAPTER 2

To the Cranberry Bogs

"As I turned after washing my vegetables through the window, I saw that there was a deer in my backyard," said Mrs. Brewster with a hand on her cheek.

She narrated this story every time she visited them from Hingham. She was a white woman in her fifties with grey hair and a kind smile.

The children and their parents nodded their heads politely.

"Have a cookie, Mrs. Brewster," their mother offered her the plate.

"Oh, lovely. Thank you," Mrs. Brewster picked one from the plate and chewed on it.

The children looked at each other with a bored expression.

They wanted to play and discuss their plan.

Yes, they had a plan, and it was the perfect time

Mother and Father were sitting on the front porch with Mrs. Brewster. They talked with her for a long time. So long that Mother forgot to say "bedtime Heather" and Father forgot to say "get settled, Davy." It was now long after bedtime.

The Children looked at each other once more and sent a silent signal.

They knew they would have time to test Heather's theory now. Her theory about the Marshwiggles.

Silently, they stood and casually walked away. It was time to execute their plan.

CHAPTER 3

The Little Adventure

Heather took little Davy firmly by the hand and quietly eased the kitchen door with her other hand.

"Where are we going, Heather?" Davy wasn't really sure.

"To find the Marshwiggles," Heather pressed her index finger to her lips before she whispered in Davy's ear.

"What?"

You see, Heather believed Grandee was telling the truth about the Marshwiggles. Mother and Father always said "nonsense" when Grandee told them stories, and sometimes only Davy believed him. After all, Davy was five and didn't know a lot of stuff as she had learned in her seven years. He hadn't even been to kindergarten yet.

But in this case, Heather was pretty sure that Marshwiggles were really possible.

"But they do not appear in front of humans. They run away, Heather," Davy reasoned.

"They helped Tyrone, Grandee's friend," Heather insisted.

"He was in distress," Davy had just learned this new word 'distress' and used it quite a lot. "Also, they ran away as soon as Tyrone was freed."

'Because they do not like grown-up humans," Heather presented another theory.

So, Heather had decided that Marshwiggles didn't like grown-ups. They couldn't know what fun Grandee really was; they'd only see he was big. But she and Davy were little, so maybe the Marshwiggles would come out if they called them and told them their names and asked them politely to play.

Davy wasn't sure, but he trusted his big sister's decision. She must be right.

The cranberry bogs weren't really far from their farm. Once they were out of the yard, they could run and skip because no one would hear them and yell that it was going to be dark soon and where were they going when they should be home in bed.

Davy said, "what can Marshwiggles play, Heather? Can they play tag or swing?"

"No, silly," replied Heather, "they have games of their own, we'll have to let them teach us their game, and then we can teach them our games."

"OK!" Davy agreed; he thought Heather was pretty smart and almost as much fun as Grandee. It would still be a few years before he scorned the company of a "girl" even though she was his big sister.

They kept walking forward. The birds chirped noisily around them as if they were winding up for the day.

The bogs were now in sight, and Heather slowed to a walk, again taking Davy's hand. They had to make their way carefully around the edges of the cranberry bogs and into the marsh.

The sun was down, but there was still lots of light as the children reached the old dead tree that stood in the marsh like a sentinel. Heather had chosen that spot because they could sit on the exposed roots and keep dry while they tried to coax the Marshwiggles to visit with them.

They made themselves comfortable, and then Davy asked, "are you gonna call them now, Heather?"

He was more than a little nervous about actually seeing Marshwiggles.

"Suppose they didn't want to be friends? "Are they very big?"

However, Heather was confident.

"They must not be big, or they wouldn't be afraid of grown-ups. Also, they are tiny people. Remember Tyrone's story?"

Davy nodded in agreement.

They were ready now.

"Hey, Marshwiggles!" She cupped her hands around her mouth.

"Hey, come out, Marshwiggles!"

"I'm Heather, and this is my little brother Davy. We thought you'd like to come and play with us!"

Both children held their breath, but there was only silence – not even a ripple in the pools of the marsh.

"Hey, Marshwiggles, we're little, and won't hurt you, come on out!"

Heather shouted her request in several different ways but with the same result – silence.

Davy was secretly relieved.

He preferred Marshwiggles from the perspective of Grandee's lap, not face to face on the roots of the old marsh tree.

The children sat and waited a while. They talked quietly; Heather told Davy how she expected to teach the Marshwiggles how to skip rope. She looked really disappointed.

Davy told Heather he thought Mother probably found out they were gone and was mad.

Heather was sure Mrs. Brewster had just gotten done talking about Mr. Brewster's last trip and was just starting to tell about what the neighbors in Hingham were doing, so Mother and Father didn't miss them yet.

Had the children been looking around, they might have caught the twinkle of a pair of golden-lashed eyes.

A young Marshwiggle was listening to their conversation and thought they were very amusing. He was very quiet and kept very still, but his eyes twinkled with suppressed laughter.

An older Marshwiggle approached him silently and, catching his eye, frowned in disapproval. Motioning with his head, he indicated they should leave the area immediately.

The youngster reluctantly followed, with another parting glance at the children.

CHAPTER 4

Oh, Come Find Us!

"Heather, it's getting dark," Davy protested, "We'd better try again tomorrow."

"Oh, little brothers!" Heather exclaimed in disgust. "You're always ready to quit," she shook her head.

But the light was beginning to fade, and they had to negotiate the cranberry bogs before they were safely on firm ground. So, she stood reluctantly and called once more.

"Hey, Marshwiggles! Last chance, you guys. We have to go home!"

There was still no answer nor any sign of life in the marsh. Heather took Davy's hand and started off toward the bogs.

Marshes are tricky in failing light, some of the grassy pools look like solid ground, and one path looks pretty much like another. Anyway, Heather didn't come out exactly where she had gone in, and both she and Davy had wet feet by the time they reached the edge of the cranberry bogs.

The bogs are nicely laid out, squared off, and separated by narrow lanes.

They were easy to walk across the single file in the light, but now, there was shadow and half-light, and the children were wet and tired.

So, naturally, the way back home seemed trickier than ever.

It really was past bedtime, and Mother and Dad had missed them and called Grandee to see if they had run over to hear a story.

After confirming with Grandee, they knew the kids were gone, which left everyone worried for them.

They began to look for the children everywhere around the farm. They checked all the places where Heather and Davy played.

"Davy, I don't see the path around the bog," Heather admitted.

"I'm afraid you'll fall if I try to lead you when I can't see.".

Davy started to cry.

"I want Mommy, Heather. Take me home."

"If we stay here," Heather reasoned, "Dad will come and look for us with the flashlight."

Heather was nervous now, but she was hopeful that their parents would soon find them.

"Father won't know where to look," Davy protested. "We didn't tell him where we were going."

With that, he really began to wail.

Heather put her arms around her little brother and tried to comfort him. She wished she had started home earlier, but she felt Father was really smart and he'd come with the light and find them, especially if they called.

"Let's yell so that Father can find us," she suggested.

Both little voices sang out together.

"Dad! Mom! we're in the marsh; come get us!" They kept yelling for help again and again with ever-shortening pauses between.

Mother and Father were becoming upset because Heather and Davy were not in any of the places they had thought to look.

Mrs. Brewster was trying to imagine where two little children could get to on a summer evening when they should be in bed.

Grandee hadn't remembered Marshwiggles yet.

The young Marshwiggle was listening to the children from a safe distance. They weren't amusing anymore because the little one was in tears, and the larger one was quite unhappy though keeping up a brave front.

"I could help them find their way," he thought. But the grown-ups had said – no contact with humans.

He paused and thought for a long moment. He was feeling really bad for the little humans. What if they were found by something else like a big animal?

He knew the rules set by the grown-ups.

Still, these humans were in trouble and obviously harmless. If there was just some way to stay out of sight, I could help them.

And BAM! it occurred to him. He could travel down the bog and call up to the children on the rim. They couldn't see him in the dark.

That felt like a fantastic idea to the little Marshwiggle. He snapped his fingers together and smiled to himself.

Fixing the hat on his tiny head, he slipped quietly past Heather and Davy and got down into the cut edge of the bog.

Then he called softly.

"Heather!"

"Davy?"

Davy stopped crying and whispered, "what was that, Heather?"

"I don't know," she answered.

"Maybe it was a Marshwiggle?" whispered Davy with his eyes wide.

The Marshwiggle called again.

"Heather, Davy?"

"Who is that?" Heather demanded.

"Are you a Marshwiggle?" Davy asked innocently.

"Yes, and if you want to get across the bog, I'll help you." the Marshwiggle answered.

"Where are you" Davy called.

"Shhh!" the Marshwiggle commanded.

"Don't let anybody know I'm helping you, and don't try to see me, ok?'

Heather peered in the direction of the voice, but since it was too dark to see anyway, she agreed. Davy was secretly relieved not to have to see a Marshwiggle just now.

The Marshwiggle guided them, giving instructions as they picked their way across, and as they reached the side of the cranberry bog next to their field, they saw a light bobbing along. Father had come searching.

"Daddy," Davy called joyfully, and he took off running. Heather was glad to see Father, but she hesitated in the hopes of catching just one glimpse of the Marshwiggle.

Father swung Davy up in his arms and hurried to Heather's side. As the light glanced across the edge of the bog, Heather caught the flash of two eyes with golden lashes.

One eye closed in a friendly wink, and then both disappeared.

ABOUT THE AUTHOR

Teressa Diggs was the wife of Lewes, the youngest of 3 siblings, and they had 5 children, one of which was a SIDS baby at 2 weeks and 2 days. The other four are all young adults with Marshwiggles of their own. She is of Swedish descent and Lewes is an African American. They home birthed 3 of the children, while the other 2 were born in a hospital. They were also advocates of homeschooling and homeschooled their 4 children for 4 years.

Teressa attended the University of Wyoming and has a Bachelor's Degree in Elementary Education, however, only used that degree to homeschool with. She was also a Librarian, telephone operator, and a youth care worker in a treatment center for troubled teens. Currently, she works from home for U-Haul Moving and Storage, which is very appropriate, as Lewes had his own moving business and was a professional mover before he passed away in 2018.

Teressa's favorite occupation was being a mother, with being a Librarian coming close behind. She loves learning and enjoyed learning new things as her children grew. She misses her children's younger days, but loves being a grandmother of 13 grandchildren and great- grandmother of at least 6, she has sort of lost count on that one. In any case, she loves children and watching them learn and grow.

Her children heard of the Marshwiggles from their Grandee, who shared the adventures with them when they were little.

Teressa's first book **Number Pattern's: In Hundred Charts** was written as a tribute to her early pet peeve which was rote learning in Math. She struggled with multiplication tables and the memorization because she moved from a school that was behind in teaching them, to a school that was ahead of learning math. She managed to make it through and even became good at math despite not knowing all those facts. She could never pass the drills but understood the concepts of numbers enough to get far in her math career.

Teressa is the oldest of four siblings and her mother was a first generation Swede who was born in Canwood, Saskatchewan in Canada. More about the author can be found at her website www.MotherhoodbyTerri.com

www.ingramcontent.com/pod-product-compliance
Lightning Source LLC
LaVergne TN
LVHW041603070526
838199LV00047B/2114